Six of Us

Written by Angie Belcher

Illustrated by Sylwia Filipczak

Collins

I am Chaz.

I can run.

This is Mum.

She can fix things.

This is Nan.

She chops the chicken.

This is Jen.

She sings to Bubs.

Dad visits us.

He has figs.

I dish up the figs.

13

/y/

14

15

After reading

Letters and Sounds: Phase 3

Word count: 39

Focus phonemes: /j/ /v/ /x/ /y/ /z/ /ch/ /sh/ /th/ /ng/

Common exception words: the, she, he, to, of, I

Curriculum links: Understanding the World: People and Communities

Early learning goals: Reading: use phonic knowledge to decode regular words and read them aloud accurately; demonstrate understanding when talking with others about what they have read

Developing fluency

- Your child may enjoy hearing you read the book.
- Model saying the speech bubble on page 13 with expression: "Yum!"

Phonic practice

- Ask your child to find all the words in the book that use the /ch/ phoneme. (*Chaz, chops, chicken*)
- Ask them to find all the words in the book that use the /th/ phoneme. (*this, things, the*)
- Look at the "I spy sounds" pages (14–15) together. Discuss the picture with your child. Can they find items/examples of words containing the /v/ and /y/ sounds? (e.g. *vest, vacuum, vase, vegetables, yacht, yo-yo, yoghurt, yellow*)

Extending vocabulary

- Ask your child:
    - What words can you think of that mean mealtime? (e.g. *dinnertime, lunchtime, teatime, suppertime*)
    - Can you think of any other words that mean **fix**? (e.g. *mend, rebuild, repair, put right*)
    - Jen says the food is **yum**. What other words could you use instead of **yum**? (e.g. *delicious, tasty, yummy, nice, lovely, scrumptious*)